p.76

family picnic

FRIENDS

ST CARD
...tion
This space for Address on...

scholar...
Pfeffernut County. Th...
fernut had high hopes for Louie.

...ft...
...mi...
...e c...

...ally thought...
... a local far...
...g basketbal...

...ot sure w...
...great thi...

Lost Toys Returned

Townspeople are delighted by the surprising return of flying discs lost on rooftops and kites tangled high in treetops. Balls and other toys long since lost began to reappear in the yards of Pfeffernut County children a few weeks back. At first, no one knew just how these things were being returned from their high places. Then a local girl spotted a lanky farmhand named Louie as he plucked two baseballs from the gutters of her family's home.

"I couldn't believe my eyes," she said. "He's nearly as tall as the water tower."

"Aw, it's nothing," Louie said. "When I see those poor toys stuck where most folks can't reach, I feel real sorry. I can't help but reach down and put them back where they belong."

Please see LOUIE, Page A2

...e
...be
...now
...e C2

Greetings from
Pfeffernut County

Grandpa at
fishing hole

Pfeffernusse Cookies — Grandma's recipe 5 dozen

4 C. flour   1/2 C. butter
1/2 tsp. ground nutmeg   1/2 tsp. cinnamon
1/2 C. white sugar   2 eggs
3/4 C. light molasses   1/2 tsp. ground cloves
1 1/4 tsp. baking soda   1/3 C. powdered sugar

Stir together flour, sugar, baking soda,
spices + dash black pepper. Melt molasses
+ butter in saucepan. Cool.
Stir in eggs, add dry ingredients
to molasses mixture, mix well, cover.
chill for several hours.
Shape into 1" balls. Place on
cookie sheet. Bake at 350°
12 to 14 minutes or until cookies
done. Cool. Roll in powdered sugar.

The Cows Cannot Mooove Along

Pfeffernut County has not seen the sun for three straight days. Weather forecasters have no idea what's going on. The local livestock is completely frozen. Cows are no longer producing milk, just ice cream. Will this deep freeze continue, or will the sun shine down on Pfeffernut again?

Pfeffernut
Book Fair $1

Pfeffernut
Book Fair $1

FARMER CAP

by Jill Kalz

illustrated by Sahin Erkocak

PICTURE WINDOW BOOKS
Minneapolis, Minnesota

Special thanks to our story consultant:
Terry Flaherty, Ph.D., Professor of English
Minnesota State University, Mankato

Editor: Christianne Jones
Designer: Tracy Davies
Page Production: Melissa Kes
Art Director: Nathan Gassman
The illustrations in this book were
created digitally.

Picture Window Books
5115 Excelsior Boulevard
Suite 232
Minneapolis, MN 55416
877-845-8392
www.picturewindowbooks.com

Library of Congress Cataloging-in-Publication Data
Kalz, Jill.
Farmer Cap / by Jill Kalz ; illustrated by Sahin Erkocak.
p. cm. — (Pfeffernut County)
Summary: After years of trying to convince their eccentric
neighbor to do things the way they do, the farmers of Pfeffernut
County finally see that Farmer Cap might have some good ideas,
after all.
ISBN-13: 978-1-4048-3139-1 (library binding)
ISBN-10: 1-4048-3139-8 (library binding)
[1. Agriculture—Fiction. 2. Eccentrics and eccentricities—Fiction.
3. Farm life—Fiction. 4. Tall tales.] I. Erkocak, Sahin, ill. II. Title.
PZ7.K12655Far 2007
[E]—dc22   2007004031

For Mom, Dad, and Mike, who sometimes think me strange but love me anyway—J.K.

Art for the farmer on County Road 27, whose plastic-wrapped hay bales inspired this story.

WELCOME TO PFEFFERNUT

Pfeffernut County is a friendly little place on the prairie. It's full of kind people who dream big. Funny things have a way of happening here. Get ready for some new adventures, and enjoy your visit. We're sure glad you stopped by.

3

Farmer Cap was a strange old man. While most farmers wore boots, he wore flip-flops. He wore shorts instead of overalls. Even though his name was Cap, he didn't own one. He always wore a hat with a long feather in it.

4

When the other farmers told jokes and laughed, Farmer Cap cried. When they complained about too much rain, Farmer Cap danced like a chicken.

Farmer Cap was a STRANGE old man.

6

When the other farmers sat and talked about crops, Farmer Cap doodled.

"What are you planting this year, Cap?" the other farmers asked. "Corn? Beans? How about peas?"

One year, Farmer Cap planted spaghetti.
The noodles grew tall in the hot sun.

8

But when it rained, the spaghetti flopped to the ground.
Harvest time was slippery, slimy work.

Last year, Farmer Cap planted Popsicle sticks. There were rows of CHERRY and ORANGE Popsicles—LIME and GRAPE ones, too.

Farmer Cap worked hard to keep them cold, but the summer sun was too hot. The colorful crops quickly turned to mud.

The other farmers told him to plant oats, beets, or strawberries.

But Farmer Cap had other ideas.

This year, Farmer Cap started planting earlier than ever.

"You'll never get a tractor through that frozen field, Cap," the other farmers said. "Wait until the snow melts, or you'll have nothing but trouble."

But Farmer Cap didn't listen. He walked up and down his field, drilling holes for his seeds. He planted late at night. The winter moon glowed full and white.

Weeks later, Farmer Cap poured syrup on the rows. The other farmers watched and scratched their heads.

"What do you think he's trying to grow?" the first farmer asked.

"I don't think it's potatoes or turnips," the second one said.

"Maybe he's growing pancakes," the third farmer said.
"Farmer Cap is a strange old man."

Winter slowly turned into spring. The other farmers started plowing their fields. They planted lettuce and carrot seeds. They planted pepper, tomato, and radish seeds, too.

The farmers smiled at the rain, and they smiled at the sun. After a while, the little seeds grew and covered the farmers' fields with green stripes.

But nothing happened to Farmer Cap's field.

One day, a truck left three giant boxes by Farmer Cap's barn. Inside were dozens of bicycle pumps. Farmer Cap filled his field with them.

The other farmers shook their heads.

"What do you think he's trying to grow?" the first farmer asked.

"I don't think it's broccoli or pumpkins," the second one said.

"That's a lot of air," the third farmer said. "He must be growing balloons."

Farmer Cap pumped air underground for weeks. His dog, Lester, even helped.

But nothing happened in the field.

Finally, one cool fall morning, the other farmers started bringing in their crops. They filled their wagons, silos, and bins.

Farmer Cap was nowhere to be seen.

Suddenly, a plane buzzed overhead. It was Farmer Cap! He flew in a loop and swooped low to the ground. A fine white powder fell on his field like snow. Some fell on the farmers, too.

"It's powdered sugar!" the farmers cried, licking their fingers.

"What is that strange old man trying to grow?"

That night, Farmer Cap couldn't sleep. If he had done everything right, tomorrow would be harvest day. He lay very still and waited.

He heard crickets chirping and an owl hooting. He heard Lester grunt in his sleep. And then, just before sunrise, Farmer Cap heard the sound he had been waiting for: **WHOOSH!**

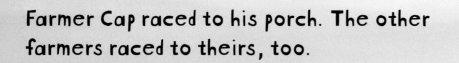

Farmer Cap raced to his porch. The other farmers raced to theirs, too.

Hundreds of giant marshmallows glowed pink in the morning light.

"Those are some prize-winners!" the first farmer said.

"I've never seen such a beautiful crop," the second one said.

"Maybe Cap could teach us a thing or two," the third farmer said. "I'd like to try something new."

From that day on, things were a little different in Pfeffernut County. Farmer Cap was still a strange old man, but the other farmers didn't notice.

They were busy growing pretzels,

donuts,

and rows of candy canes.

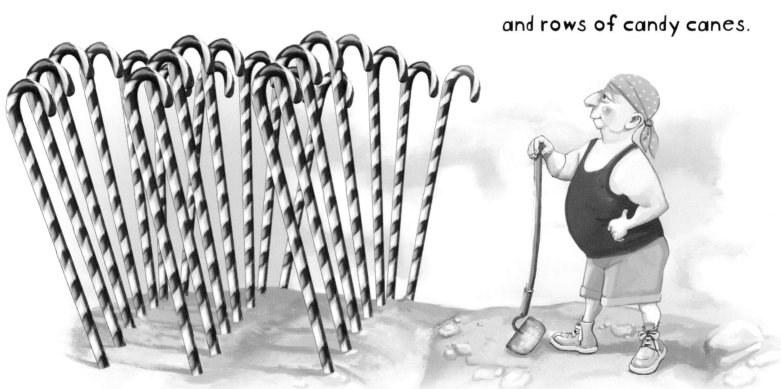

PFEFFERNUT FOLLOW-UP

1. Farmer Cap has his own style. He doesn't dress or act like the other farmers. In what ways are you different from your friends? In what ways are you alike?

2. All of the other farmers want Farmer Cap to plant a normal crop, such as corn, beans, or peas. But Farmer Cap chooses to plant an unusual crop, instead. When is it a good idea to do what everyone else does? When is it a good idea not to? Give examples.

3. Farmer Cap's spaghetti flops. His Popsicles melt. If you were a farmer and could grow anything in the world, what would it be? Chocolate chips? Blueberry muffins? String cheese? What kinds of problems might you have?

4. Even though his spaghetti and Popsicle crops fail, Farmer Cap doesn't give up. He tries again. And his next crop is a success! Describe a time when you struggled but didn't give up.

5. Throughout the story, the other farmers ask, "What do you think he's trying to grow?" What did you think Farmer Cap was trying to grow? Why?

6. Would you want to be Farmer Cap? Why or why not?

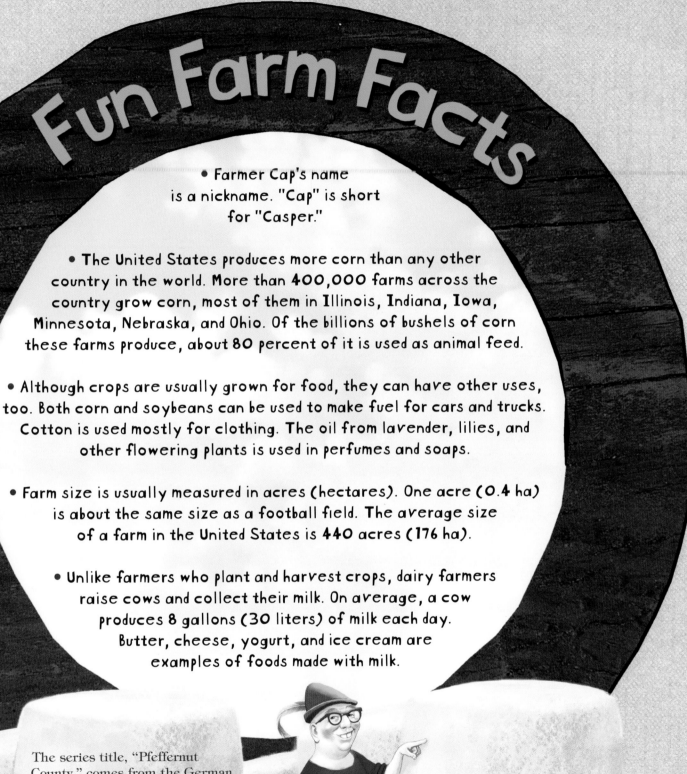

Fun Farm Facts

• Farmer Cap's name is a nickname. "Cap" is short for "Casper."

• The United States produces more corn than any other country in the world. More than 400,000 farms across the country grow corn, most of them in Illinois, Indiana, Iowa, Minnesota, Nebraska, and Ohio. Of the billions of bushels of corn these farms produce, about 80 percent of it is used as animal feed.

• Although crops are usually grown for food, they can have other uses, too. Both corn and soybeans can be used to make fuel for cars and trucks. Cotton is used mostly for clothing. The oil from lavender, lilies, and other flowering plants is used in perfumes and soaps.

• Farm size is usually measured in acres (hectares). One acre (0.4 ha) is about the same size as a football field. The average size of a farm in the United States is 440 acres (176 ha).

• Unlike farmers who plant and harvest crops, dairy farmers raise cows and collect their milk. On average, a cow produces 8 gallons (30 liters) of milk each day. Butter, cheese, yogurt, and ice cream are examples of foods made with milk.

The series title, "Pfeffernut County," comes from the German word *Pfeffernuesse* (FEFF-er-noos). Pfeffernuesse are German spice cookies that are popular around Christmastime. They get their spicy flavor from ingredients such as cinnamon, nutmeg, cloves, and black pepper.

More Books to Read

Barrett, Judi. *Cloudy with a Chance of Meatballs.* New York: Atheneum, 1978.

Cowley, Joy. *Mrs. Wishy-Washy's Farm.* New York: Philomel Books, 2003.

Krosoczka, Jarrett J. *Punk Farm.* New York: Alfred A. Knopf, 2005.

Kutner, Merrily. *Down on the Farm.* New York: Holiday House, 2004.

Waddell, Martin. *Farmer Duck.* Cambridge, Mass.: Candlewick Press, 1992.

FactHound

FactHound offers a safe, fun way to find Web sites realted to topics in this book. All of the sites on FactHound have been researched by our staff.

1. Visit *www.facthound.com*
2. Type in this special code: 1404831398
3. Click on the FETCH IT button.

Your trusty FactHound will fetch the best sites for you!

Look for all of the books in the Pfeffernut County series:

Farmer Cap
Fawn Braun's Big City Blues
Henry Shortbull Swallows the Sun
Louie the Layabout

32